Sunset in the Mists - The Dark Draws the Curtain

The Evynsford Chronicles, Volume 1

Julianne T. Grey

Published by Imaginarium Press Publishing, 2018.

This is a work of fiction. Similarities to real people, places, or events are entirely coincidental.

SUNSET IN THE MISTS - THE DARK DRAWS THE CURTAIN

First edition. April 9, 2018.

Copyright © 2018 Julianne T. Grey.

ISBN: 978-1987654011

Written by Julianne T. Grey.

Also by Julianne T. Grey

The Evynsford Chronicles
Sunset in the Mists - The Dark Draws the Curtain
Midnight in the Mists - The Dark Deepens
Dawn in the Mists - The Dark Breaks
Lost in the Mists
Found in the Mists

Prologue: Any Port In A Storm

Churning waves, black and grey, crested under the cloud-choked night skies, beating upon the coast with a perpetual dull roar. Not to be outdone, the wind keened sharply over the rocky shores, shaving the peaks of the waves to cast the salty foam far and wide. The sea surged again, a dull brute pounding out its frustration with another grinding roar and ponderous blow. The black rocks glistened in silent, stalwart mockery of both wind and wave.

It was not a night to be out and about upon the battered shoals, yet no one had told the town of Evynsford.

Like stubborn barnacles, patches of low, rough-hewn homes dotted the craggy slope where inlet became scrubby hills and ridges. Windows, mean and hooded, stabbed out with warm light escaping between the slats of their latched shutters. Most of the homes, thatch topped and daubed rock, glowered at the sea with their beetled brows. The old church and commerce house, sturdier and well-cut edifices, stood taller, their slate-tiled peaks daring the storm. The hamlet had born nights like these, what locals often referred to as a "biter" on account of what seemed to be the predominant intention of the weather toward human flesh, for thousands of nights since its foundation nearly four hundred years before. By now, the bleak March of 1898, such a "biter" was hardly worth noting.

That being said, not a soul seemed to have any pressing business to draw them out of their homes.

In the Flat-Sole, the local establishment of all matters alcoholic and domestic, many a man would be spending the night "gettin' bit", expecting to emerge the next drizzly morning with red-rimmed eyes to stagger down the boards marking the safest path from where the town squatted to the jetties and piers. They would have a look to their boats and trawling nets, and many expected they would have to spend a whole day patching and mending after this storm, for as more than one fellow observed that night, "This 'uns got some teef to it."

What they would find the next morning would drive every last thought of "bitten" nets and fishing skiffs out of their liquor-battered minds.

That night, the "biter" had spit something back out upon the jagged beach.

DONALD MOPPED AT HIS face and struggled admirably to force his brain into action. His struggle was not aided by the remnants of all the previous night's pints swilling around inside his skull.

He had just managed to drag the question from his soggy wits when Roger Blakes gasped it out at his elbow.

"Where the devil did that come from?"

The two men stood upon the slick boards of the Evynsford dock, staring at the splintered prow of the large cutter which had been driven to rest jaggedly upon the shattered blanks of the main pier. Its two large square-sails hung in flayed tatters over its riven decks, some slapping limply against the ruptured hull as its masts, cracked and listing, swung dangerously off center. Not a sign of her crew remained, though the snapped lines trailing across her deck bore a kind of grim, mute testimony.

There in the thick mists and pallid morning light, the ruined vessel could almost be mistaken for some kind of primordial leviathan vomited from a disgusted sea to impale its bulk upon the boards and piers it had splintered upon its descent. For a handful of heartbeats, Donald and Roger stood gaping dumbly as Roger's bewildered question hung over the fallen vessel.

Another voice, younger and sharper than Roger's, broke the moment of stunned perplexity.

"Oi! Lads, look!" came the shrill call of Sammy Daws behind the pair.

Donald and Roger met each other's eyes as Daws made his catapulting proclamation.

"Salvage!"

Donald and Roger, long-time mates and neither of them a friend to that loud-mouthed rip Sammy Daws, began to scramble over the fractured boards toward the ruined cutter. There was salvage to be had, and the first man to lay hold of it took the claim! Time-honored and legally enshrined precepts held that in cases such as this, the contents of a storm-wrecked vessel were open to any who could lay hold of them. Neither of the two men planned to let the likes of Daws and his cronies make off with what they had been the first to find.

Their bodies involuntarily groaning at the sudden demands placed upon them, the seasoned fishermen dragged themselves on board the creaking deck of the cutter. As Donald hoisted himself aboard, he spied the cracked lettering scrawled across her shivered bough.

HMS *Tiresias*

This might have sparked some vague, archaic memory in the fisherman's mind had he not been recovering from a "gettin' bit" and also had he not used the face of another eager salvager to propel himself up over the rail from which he had been hanging.

Standing aboard the ship, the two mates shared another quick look and then nodded to each other.

"Hold," Roger called over his shoulder as he made for the portal leading into the cutter's belly.

"Cabin," Donald answered as he picked his way to the back of the ship, avoiding the worst of the crack-riddled deck as he waved trailing lines away like sodden jungle vines. He could hear other men beginning to scramble aboard the groaning craft, and he had to fight the urge to rush wildly toward the cabin.

"More haste, less speed, Donnie," he reminded himself aloud.

He heard the sharp snap of wood and then a breathless curse before a loud splash.

With an ugly grin, Donald hoped it was Sammy Daws.

At last he was moving past the helm toward the cabin door, which even then seemed to loom so large in his eyes. Already he began to imagine all the fine things he might find within; a stuffed lockbox, a fancy timepiece, some ridiculously expensive officer curios, a stash of princely liquors. All Donald's many hard years dragging a living from the miserly sea came to a glorious fulfillment on this day!

These dreamy visions vanished when a hard hand clutched at his leg.

Donald cried out and lurched backward. The grip clung to his trousers with a numb, desperate strength.

SUNSET IN THE MISTS - THE DARK DRAWS THE CURTAIN

The fisherman looked down into a face, perhaps once handsome and noble, now left an utter ruin to match the ship which bore its owner. Torn, raw and bruised, the man must have been in agony near to death from the travail of his vessel's beaching upon the Evynsford dock. For all this, though, it was not the ragged and mortally wounded nature of the man which squeezed another scream from the naturally stoic Donald.

Where the man's eyes should have been were nothing but puckered craters, the welts and blisters about which hinted at their recent, fiery removal.

The man was saying something, but Donald could not hear until after he had run out of wind from screaming.

"...saw them, before they took them," the man raved as he lay beside the helm, clutching at Donald's legs. "Before they took my, my, m-m-my, oh God, help me, my eyes!"

The last words were a wracking sob.

"Saw what?" Donald asked breathlessly.

"Little shackles!" the man shrieked, surging upward, grabbing at Donald's shirtfront. "I saw him with little collars and tiny shackles!"

Then the wretch gave a wracking cough and collapsed upon the deck. As blood leaked from between his limp, ragged lips, Donald finally noticed the jagged spar jutting from the man's back.

Chapter 1: A Vision of Dry Bones

Inspector Arthur Eldermann gave only the softest grunt of discomfort as he emerged from the hackney coach, unfolding his tall frame with the languorous yet glorious stretch of any sojourner who has spent too long in an uncomfortable position.

His stretch complete with a slow sigh, he took Evynsford in with a single, cold glance to match the stinging wind about him and the grey sky overhead. The look on his face did nothing to disguise his thoughts on the scene before him.

What a wretched waste of my time, he thought as he watched the crisp sea breeze tickle at the skirts of the thatched roofs.

The coachman was staggering, stiff-legged, down from his perch and made a show of undoing the straps in the back which held Inspector Eldermann's singular beaten travel bag. Apparently, the weathered fellow was under the delusion that his belaboring would inspire some open-handed gratitude from Preston's finest and fiercest inspector.

"You were paid by the Constable's Office, yes?" Eldermann queried over his shoulder as he turned to regard the shoals below the town and the ramshackle dock, all shrouded in heavy coils of fog.

"Eh, yes," the coachman grunted as he took the bag from its mount at last. "I been paid to take ye hear, and when I receive post from ye I'm to come to fetch ye back."

SUNSET IN THE MISTS - THE DARK DRAWS THE CURTAIN

Eldermann turned from his disparaging glances over the foggy seaside and archly regarded the squat man bearing his bag.

"Post?" he said so evenly it almost hid the edge in his tone. "Am I to assume that your station's offices have not discovered the telegraph?"

"Assume what ye like," the man huffed churlishly, his hopes of generosity swallowed by his irritation at the Inspector's condescension. "But we gots a telegraph at the station sure enough, but t'ain't a rail or telegraph station anywhere here abouts. You'd have to ride near to the distance back to Preston just to find one."

Eldermann took the bag brusquely from the man and gave a confirming, if resigned, nod.

"Very well, then, the post."

"Post goes out once a week, on a Thursday," the coachman said flatly, though he couldn't keep a wicked grin from tugging at the corner of his mouth. "I'll be about the following Monday."

"With all speed, I am sure," Eldermann remarked coolly and then began to head toward the village with the coachman chuckling thickly as he clambered back aboard his hackney.

Coming from the village, the chill gusts tugging at what hair remained on his pale pate, was a stumpy and lumpen man who could have been a distant cousin to the departing coachman. A broad, limp-brimmed hat was clutched in one hand, the other shoved deep into the pockets of the oiled leather coat flapping about his thumping boots.

"You are Watchman Douglas Buie," the Inspector pronounced without slowing as he neared the obviously nervous man. "Here to introduce me to the case and your lovely little town."

"Yes, eh – pleasure to meet ye, Inspector." Buie bobbed his head and tried to extend a hand of greeting only to realize he had forgotten that the proffered hand was still rammed into his pocket. He struggled to emancipate his hand before realizing that Inspector Eldermann had not slowed. With another set of his long, quick strides, he was past the floundering watchman.

"There are still no bodies, correct?" Eldermann asked as Buie rushed to catch up.

"Eh, no, thank God, not yet," Buie called as he struggled to match the taller man's ground-devouring gait, his doughy cheeks flushing with the effort. "But there is somefing ye must know, Inspector."

"Oh, I wouldn't thank him so quickly," Eldermann chided as they neared the outermost building, the gravel here fresher than the mud-clogged stuff of the road. It crunched crisply under their boots.

"If we had a body, we might actually have some evidence of a crime."

Buie blanched at that, something remarkable given his natural pallor, the former blush fleeing in light of the current circumstances.

"Master Eldermann," the watchman huffed in part-shock, part-exertion. "The children they, well – eh, they is..."

"Yes, yes, I am sure I am being insensitive, but you must understand that a few children running off seems a rather small thing when we consider I was working a rather gruesome and fascinating rash of-"

"All!" Buie barked sharp and hard enough to cut through sound, wave and wind.

Eldermann stopped and turned sharply on his heel to stare down at the quivering man.

"Pardon?" he said in a voice grown weighty with earnestness.

"T'ain't a few children, Inspector," Watchman Buie nearly panted, both hands wringing his hat. "Tis all, ye see. Every last child who's been walking a spell but not seen their thirteenth year be gone."

Inspector Eldermann stood very still for a moment, his gaze resting heavily on the squirming Buie while the wind whistled between them.

"Now that," Eldermann said, a smile teased upon his lips. "That could be something interesting."

THEY WERE NOW WALKING down the crushed rock streets, Buie having just finished explaining, albeit haltingly, the unfolding events.

At first the vanishings had been only a few incidents separated by weeks. Worrisome, yes, especially in such a small community, but nothing extraordinary. Then things began to escalate. The time between disappearances shrank, and sometimes more than one child was taken in a single incident. Parents and children became terror-stricken, and a closer and closer watch was kept over every youth thirteen or younger, as that pattern at least was discerned. It was all for naught, though, as the tighter the parents held their children, the quicker they disappeared. The last quartet of children had been taken, all from different homes, from underneath their parents' noses, in one night a ten-day ago.

"And no one has ever been able to confirm seeing a person or persons about during the disappearances?"

Eldermann scanned the cluster of low homes on either side of the road leading to what passed for a town square.

"Not but shadows and fleetin' shapes in the dark or fog," Buie answered, glaring at the offending mist which even now seemed to cast everything in a ghostly spectrum despite the whistling wind.

Now this might be something worth my time, the Inspector let himself think as his mind began to work at a feverish pitch.

"Curious," Eldermann mused. "I will need to conduct interviews and inspections, of each family and the locations where each child was last seen, respectively."

"Well, as to the families, ye are sure as goin' to be meetin' 'em soon," Buie said in a tone which suggested he did not envy Eldermann's fate.

"All in good time," the Inspector replied distractedly as they stepped onto the roughly square plain of crude flagstones that stretched before a steepled church, a stolid commerce house, and a rambling tavern. "However, first I will need to stow my effects and have a drink where I am being lodged."

"That'd be the Flat-Sole, Inspector," Buie said with a nod to the tavern. "And that also be what I mean, Inspector. They're all there."

"Who?" Eldermann asked, emerging from his thoughts as his boot heels clipped on the stone.

"The families," Buie said gravely. "They knew ye'd be stayin' here and so they all come to see ye."

Inspector Eldermann stood a few paces away from the tavern. His eyes saw the dark, seething mass of shapes moving behind the grimy glass of the tavern windows. Even from outside, the babble of so many voices seemed like a growling beast in its lair.

"I hate small places," Eldermann sighed, giving Buie a knowing look. "Small places and small people."

Buie stared back blankly. Eldermann sucked in a breath with a hiss and then went to the tavern door.

Chapter 2: A Light Under a Bowl

Regina Hollferd watched the constable step inside the Flat-Sole, just before everyone began to holler and jabber at once. She had the briefest impression of a tall, lean man with rich, dark hair swept back from his neatly groomed face.

Then everyone was standing and mobbing toward the door, desperate to be the first to receive the constable's attention.

As though that will bring the children back any quicker, Regina thought with genuine sorrow instead of spite. *How these mothers must suffer, oh Father, how all of Evynsford suffers.*

Dolores Moss shouldered past her. The lines drawn ragged upon the face of the woman nearly five years her junior were the surest of confirmations.

Evynsford was suffering.

The disappearances ... no, the abductions, for what else could they be ... had begun nearly three months ago when Betsy Moss, a girl of eleven, was not found in her bed when her mother went to wake her for her morning chores. While the disappearance of anyone, especially a child, was noticeable in the small community, it was known that Betsy was a willful child and prone to wandering far a-field when her mother was not looming over her. The aged and superstitious murmured toothlessly of "Wee People" and "Fair Folk" making away with rebellious children, but most just shook their heads at such nonsense. The majority thought at best that the girl had wandered away at night and would be found within a few days, or at worst that she had wandered off and some terrible fate had befallen her. After all, it was not the first time the sea cliffs and dark hills had claimed a foolhardy child.

The crowd in the Flat-Sole seemed to seethe and lap about the door, a fleshy imitation of the sea beyond, and then the constable cut through the human waves like a tall-masted sloop under full sail. Sharp and dark, he briskly shouldered past baying fathers and keening mothers, a battered travel bag held in one long hand.

He pressed toward the bar, implacable and almost radiating a chilly air as he moved closer to where she sat upon a long-legged stool. This cold aura struck Regina smartly as she saw him advance and watched his face. His features, fierce, almost lupine in severity, showed none of the bewilderment or concern that would be expected of a man suddenly swamped with the yowling mob of Evynsford's bereaved parents. He did not even seem angry or afraid, which also might have made some sense to her. Instead, all she saw was a kind of cool intent, like the face of a practiced artisan bending over his tools for yet another labor. A hint of pride arched his dark brows over grey-green eyes that showed none of the scorn which haunted the almost sneering lips framed by his immaculate moustache and beard.

Regina Hollferd, who had long practice in perceiving the hearts of men, whispered a prayer that was quickly swallowed by the braying crowd: "My Lord and Father, who have you sent us? What man can look on these broken people with nothing but ice and disdain on his face?"

The constable was at the bar now, setting his bag beneath the counter and rummaging in his coat pocket with his free hand. He said something to Jimmy Howe, the barkeep, but Jimmy only shook his head to set his jowls to flapping and gestured at the thundering crowd pressing in even louder upon their now-stationary target. The constable gave the man a heavy glare – oh, Regina nearly shivered at the weight of it – and then fetched out a trio of coins upon the bar from his pocket. Without pause, he took a tumbler and bottle of brandy from behind the bar, his long limbs putting both in easy reach.

Jimmy flushed and began to bark something at the man, who merely shook his head and gestured to the crowd around him as he filled the tumbler.

The constable began to turn back to the crowd, liquor in hand. In the sweep of his pivot, he and Regina met eye to eye.

A distant but not unfamiliar thrill traced its way down Regina's back to nest warmly in her belly as those unflinching, crushing eyes seemed to rest on her. He saw her, and there was a potency, an intimacy in that moment of truly being seen. The thrill became a flutter of tentative excitement and, yes, fear as she bore that lingering look.

Then one lid slid over one of those winnowing eyes, a teasing wink, before his gaze left her and he turned to face the crowd, tossing back a mouthful of brandy.

Regina let out an indignant huff. *What cheek!*

Whatever magic he once had was so thoroughly broken with that roguish gesture that Regina felt heat coming to her cheeks in a rush of outrage and embarrassment. She felt slighted, perhaps a little cheapened, and experienced a fresh dislike for this swaggering, sneering officer of the law.

SUNSET IN THE MISTS - THE DARK DRAWS THE CURTAIN

What kind of man, indeed.

The constable began to say something which the howling crowd drowned out. Then he raised his head and his words reverberated with a deep-voiced power.

"Kindly shut your mouths," he bellowed. "Now!"

Shockingly, the crowd began to quiet. Not all at once, but within a minute they had all fallen silent under the constable's icy stare.

"Good," he said softly, as if checking their commitment to the silence, before taking another hearty drink. "I am Inspector Eldermann, sent here upon your request from Preston Constabulary Offices. Mister Buie has more or less informed me of the situation here in Evynsford, that being your children's disappearances-"

"Kidnappin'!" came a shrill cry from Maggie Cook. It seemed the storm might erupt again, but Inspector Eldermann's glare quieted them with a pummeling sweep.

"Disappearances," Eldermann said with sharp, challenging articulation. "I will continue to use this term because as things stand we know absolutely nothing about the where, the why or the how they have gone. Fear and useless speculation are matters for the church, not police work."

Regina winced a bit at the bite in that barb. *What sort of man?*

"Heresy," someone growled in the crowd, and a few people rumbled their agreement. Regina questioned the exact prognosis, but shared the general sentiment

"Actually, that falls more squarely in the realm of blasphemy. Trust me, I would know."

The last words drew a small smile across his face, something made ugly with bitterness. To her shock, Regina saw that twisted smirk and felt nothing but pity for its bearer.

What dagger does that smile hide, and what put it there in the first place?

More grumbles broke out, but Inspector Eldermann was having none of it.

"Do you people want your children found or would you rather have a theological debate?" he nearly snarled, showing the first sign of actual temper.

Silence ruled again.

"Very good," he said archly before a final draining tip of the tumbler, which he slammed down on the bar hard enough to make many, especially Jimmy, wince. "Now, once I am settled into my rooms I will be drafting an interview and inspection schedule with Mister Buie. I will speak with each of you in proper course, and I will not stop my investigations until I have found every last child. On that point you can be certain."

Despite themselves, several reluctant murmurs of approval escaped the scowling crowd.

"You will not like me, I can nearly guarantee that. I am a hard, unsympathetic and thoroughly irreverent man. I do not care about your sensitivities, your customs or your superstitions, and you can expect that I will defy and disrespect them all in turn as I prosecute my search."

A brittle silence returned.

"But you can must understand two things. First is that I am very, very good at what I do. I am the best chance you have of finding those missing. Second, and this is perhaps even more important, is that I know for a fact that I am the only one Preston plans to send for the foreseeable future. So, it seems I am also the only hope you have."

The faces of the gathered parents created a battlefield of hope, fear and desperation.

Silently, head bowed, Regina said another earnest prayer.

Father, what man have you sent?

Chapter 3: A Valley of Shadow

Inspector Arthur Eldermann mopped at his face and then turned back to survey one more time the ravine that ran behind the Julep home. The stone and green grass were dark and slick with the wet of the fog that slithered between the arms of the parallel ridges. He had nearly bashed his brains out when he had clambered down into that narrow defile and slipped upon those jagged, slippery rocks. Even then, hands bloodied and trousers gouged, he had nothing to show for his inspections.

No sign of the Juleps' twin sons. No evidence of a dark shape passing down the ravine. Nothing. Nothing but the damned fog and the constant groan of the blasted Irish Sea which lay less than a quarter mile down the ravine.

Sea and fog and nothing.

Inspector Eldermann knew that he was not nice or a gentleman, but with one glaring, ancient exception he did not consider himself an angry man. Often insensitive, regularly curt and occasionally brutish, yes, yes and yes, but angry – no. Anger would cost him too much, require too much of his essence, for he had learned to despise the term "soul" and all its trappings, and the one thing he was determined to not give away was any part of himself. At least, not any true part of what he was.

Cursing bitterly, viciously, he turned on his heel and began to trudge his way back up toward where the Julep homestead lay, or where he believed it was, for the fog had made even that short distance into a maddening kaleidoscope of vague shapes, rippling silhouettes and evasive shadows.

As he marched back, his boots making a thudding squelch in the sodden ground, he reflected on why his anger bedeviled him so.

It was not that he hadn't had difficult cases before. He had actually taken on the more obscure, esoteric and confounding cases that came tumbling through the Constable's Office. He liked keeping busy and savored throwing himself into a puzzling case. He enjoyed it so much that he had done some consulting via correspondence with other agencies and offices from various communities across the country. There was that "bloofer" business a few years ago, and then professional consultations for a Doctor Laythem, or was it Layton, before that. The point was predisposed toward the elusive and macabre. So why did this case infuriate him so when, indeed, as several of the boys back at the Office were prone to say when a case took a queer turn, "This one's got Brother Eldermann all over it"?

He passed within the garden gate and began to make his way around the mist-wrapped home, his teeth flashing as he remembered the despised appellation of his colleagues. He supposed he was glad they had stopped calling him Father Eldermann, though that had come at the cost of Constable Burns's nose and a formal reprimand. Still, Brother Eldermann was only a marginal improvement.

He already knew how much of his life he had wasted without those thick gob-smackers dredging it up all the time.

He cleared the house and was making for his borrowed horse by the roadside hitching post when Missus Katherine Julep trundled out the front door and called after him.

"Constable Eldermann," she yelped shrilly, kicking a leg free of one of her clinging children with an unintelligible snarl.

Eldermann stopped, feeling his body stiffen, but then with a steadying breath he turned to regard the mother of the missing twins.

"Inspector, madam," he said without greeting or preamble, but still trying to keep his tone level. "It is Inspector Eldermann. A constable is for when you need a vagrant tossed or a footpad trounced. An inspector is for when you need to know something. It may seem a mere formality, but I ask that you try and remember it. Particularly as it is on your behalf that I am inspecting."

Katherine Julep, a babe pinned to her hip with one thick arm, gave *Inspector* Eldermann a sour look, but it quickly passed into one of the most pitiable crestfallen-ness.

"Ye 'aven't found no sign of me boys, 'ave ye," she stated, no actual question in her voice.

The Julep twins were the second disappearance, neither of them returning one night after attending to their chore of disposing of night-soil by the seashore. Real, living hope had died inside their world-weary mother during the second month of their absence. Only its specter, conjured by maternal instinct, remained.

"Nothing definitive or seemingly useful at the moment," Inspector Eldermann conceded as he began moving toward the hitching post again. "But it is another piece to the puzzle, and in the end even the most mundane could be important."

The tawny-coated mare, loaned him by one of the families on whose behalf he now worked, turned a wet, placid eye to Eldermann as he began to untie her.

The woman seemed unimpressed with his answer. "Sounds like a fancy way o' sayin' ye got no idea as to what's goin' on."

It seemed Missus Julep shared the mare's assessment.

"I know just what is going on," the Inspector said coolly before hoisting himself up into the saddle.

Katherine Julep, her motherly nature sparked to attention, looked up at him sharply. Again, that wraith of desperate hope danced behind her small, bloodshot eyes.

"There are children missing and I must find them," he said simply, impassively watching her will crumble a little more. "How much simpler could it be."

"Ye're a roight foul git," she spat and rotated the babe, who had begun fuss, to her other hip. "Teasin' a grievin' mother loike that. Haven't ye any heart?"

"It is my mind which makes me useful to you, Missus Julep," he called over his shoulder as he set the horse to trotting. "And last I knew, no one's lot was much improved because of their heart."

With Missus Julep wagging her head behind him, Inspector Eldermann moved down the road and into the mist.

Chapter 4: A Lot Cast in a Lap

Regina Hollferd walked down the road, arms full of wrapped parcels, lips laden with prayers.
Loving God,
Her footsteps click on the gravel, a steady rhythm to match the cadence of her skirts flapping in the wind. Its constancy and certainty were traits she wished the Holy Spirit would lay across her troubled soul.
Your Son told his disciples
These past three months had been a long string of sleepless nights and weary, oppressed days. In those long watches and endless hours, she had turned to God's Holy Word and her prayer hymnals. Though they eased the aching hours, it was a fleeting respite from a battle that seemed without end.
To become like little children
When Betsy had disappeared, even with all the gossip mongering, Regina knew something was deeply wrong. It was not just because as the county schoolmistress she knew that Betsy, notorious for her willfulness, was actually just a very intelligent young girl who had not yet mastered her tongue – two nearly unforgivable traits in the provincial little hamlet. Betsy may have been presumptuous but she was neither foolhardy nor mean-spirited enough to simply run off. Rumors of her nightly excursions greatly exaggerated. Even still, it was not that knowledge alone,

but the heavy weight that settled over her heart when the fog rolled in. The girl disappearing only confirmed what Regina had somehow known.

Lead us to work for the welfare

As more and more of the chairs in her little schoolhouse fell empty, it was as if the spiritual noose had tightened. At nights Regina would rise from her bed in the small residence adjoining the schoolhouse, gasping for air. Falling to her knees beside her bed, feeling nothing but the black night pressing in on her, she would cry out with earnest supplication for God's help, and then because their faces bubbled up in her mind in that darkness, she would pray for the missing children with wheezing, hitching breaths until she could breathe once more and collapse into oblivious sleep.

And protection of all children

Then one day no children came to the schoolhouse, their parents forbidding them to leave their sight, but it had not spared them. She had gone to Vicar Weston and together they had planned times to go and pray over those children not yet taken, and to bring food and words of encouragement to those already stricken. Some had welcomed them, others were coldly disposed, and more than a few were so numb with grief that Regina doubted they had heard anything said to them. One, Mister Kulver, a widower whose young daughter had been the fourth or fifth child taken, had become enraged when they offered prayers and had frightened Regina as he scattered the loaves of bread she had brought, cursing her bitterly. She had left quickly, near tears as he screamed incoherent profanity after her, but that night she prayed feverishly for Mister Kulver and his daughter.

We ask this in the name of Your Son

Now with every child gone, there were none left to pray over but so many to console and bring food to. With no children to teach, she had taken to baking most of the morning and then traveling about the town and the more far-flung homes bringing bread or biscuits along with her heartfelt prayers all the afternoon. She would talk with the families, and many were the hands she held, and often her collar was wet with mournful tears. Sometimes those tears were not just those of the bereft families, and heavy were her steps at twilight as she walked back to the empty schoolhouse.

Jesus Christ

More recently many of those she met had taken to speaking of the constable – no, inspector, he was quite specific on that point – and the flurry of interviews and investigations he had made in the last ten-day he had been in Evynsford. All seemed to agree he was a clever but utterly heartless man, though they clung to the hope that this ruthlessness would bring their children home. What else could they hope for?

Amen

Not for the first or last time, Regina Hollferd, felt her entire soul cry out to God upon that mist-blanketed road, desperate for some assurance, some sign that she was heard.

"Amen!" she called to God and the swallowing fog. "Amen and let it be so!"

Silence, as deep and mournful as what ruled her hollowed schoolroom, answered her.

SUNSET IN THE MISTS - THE DARK DRAWS THE CURTAIN

SHE WAS HALFWAY TO the Kulver farmhouse, against Vicar Weston's fervent admonishments, when Regina heard the peculiar cadence of hooves galloping upon gravel-pocked earth.

This was more than a little unusual considering that horses were rare in the hamlet and those farms or more affluent families that may have possessed them used them almost exclusively as draft animals. Such a heavy-footed, burdened beast would not be galloping down the road.

Not unless one of those owners had need to rush to his neighbor, such as in the case of an accident or remarkable discovery, such as when the wreck had struck upon the Evynsford dock nearly four months ago. Indeed, news of that hulk had spread like wildfire and the entire vessel had been scavenged and stripped, even its boards cannibalized, inside of a week.

What could spark such haste, she wondered, and then her heart leapt – the children!

Could someone have found the children or at least some sign of them?

The hoofbeats drew closer. She moved to the very skirt of the roadway and waited.

To her surprise, the galloping seemed to be slowing as it approached her, until soon the horse must have been moving at a tentative canter. She very much doubted that whoever it was could have seen her from so far off, as she could only just then make out the shape of a horse and rider plowing through the cloaking curls of mist. The figure seemed to have stopped just beyond the edge of recognition, a looming silhouette.

For an instant, she felt very small and vulnerable, a lone woman upon a mist-shrouded road with a spectral horseman seeming intent on standing sentinel over her for some unknown purpose. She was surreptitiously rearranging her wrapped parcels of baking within her basket so she could hurl one at the phantom if need be when, suddenly enough to make her jump and spill all the aforementioned burdens, a stream of blistering curses cut the air.

Half of the profanity was of such incredible potency and vitriol that she was not even sure she knew what the words meant, but the deep, clear tones left little doubt in her mind about who sat upon that idle horse.

Hands on hips, Regina called out in her sharpest schoolhouse rebuke, cutting off the tirade mid-syllable.

"Well, that certainly is not how young men should speak in general, and in the presence of the fairer sex in particular."

The rider nudged his mount forward and Inspector Eldermann emerged astride a tawny old mare. He looked down upon Regina standing on the side of the road, her parcels strewn about her, and there was a cold turn to his lips that could not be called a smile.

"My apologies, Miss, I had not expected to find fairer members of our species upon this blasted road. Now, where might they be, eh?"

Regina's cheeks reddened and her stare became as stony as the hills about them.

"Going to and fro upon the earth, and walking up and down it, I suppose," she replied icily.

"Ha." He laughed in what might have been the first actual show of good humor she had ever seen from him. "Job chapter one, verse seven."

Regina was surprised at the easily cited reference, but not so shocked that she did not notice the grimace, almost of pain or perhaps despair, which swept across the Inspector's face.

"Ahem, anyway," the Inspector mumbled, clearing his throat. "I was heading to the Kulver farm to have a walk about the grounds, and it seems I am not sure as to whether I am heading in the right direction or not."

For the briefest instant she considered sending the disagreeable man off in the wrong direction, but no sooner had the thought crossed her mind then she dismissed it as petulant and wasteful. Weren't there children to find?

"Well, your doubt is wasted," she said with a sigh as she bent to pick up her parcels. "You are on the right road, and as long as you don't turn from it you should reach the Kulver farm inside of an hour. Far less if you keep the frantic speed you had when I first heard you."

"Should have known better than to have doubted myself," Eldermann groused, more as a reproach to himself than a statement to her, for all its boastful implication. "I have wasted enough time on second guessing anyhow."

He stared down at her, his eyes seeing her and yet swimming with thoughts she could not and would not guess at.

"If you say so," she intoned with what she hoped was a tactful hint of dismissal. It seemed she had done an exemplary job of scattering her packaged baking, and it was no mean task to gather them off the gravel and skirt of grass beside the road. She wished he would take his leave and let her stoop about without feeling like a bug under a glass.

"You were at the Flat-Sole when I first arrived," the Inspector remarked abruptly, leaning forward in the saddle. "You were there, but you weren't one of the wailing mothers pawing at me as soon as I walked through the door."

"A very keen observation," she remarked frostily, the memory of his cheeky wink causing her courtesy to grow brittle.

"Either you were there on an afternoon to begin your drinking or you had some reason besides motherly grief to be concerned about the children of Evynsford," Eldermann said with no small hint of self-satisfaction. "In either case, I suppose you should be congratulated, either for your later charity of spirit or your former ability to not look like a degenerate drunk."

Regina Hollferd reared back up smartly, feeling a surprising heat in her chest that flew to her mouth.

"Is this how you speak to the families whom you are supposed to be serving?" she snapped, her parcels forgotten in the face of this cad's insufferable rudeness. "If so, I can hardly be surprised that you have been here a ten-day without no scrap of progress to show for it. Now, why don't you roll down the road and share some of your barbarous observations with Mister Kulver. I am sure he would love to hear them as he cries and clutches his daughter's favorite poppet."

The Inspector lapsed into silence again, in thought or humiliation she did not know or very much care. Regina drew in a shuddering breath to still the heat which still throbbed angrily in her chest. Then she went back to collecting her parcels into the broad basket held at her hip.

She heard the creak of saddle leather and the crunch of gravel.

Please, Heavenly Father, please just let this man leave me be.

SUNSET IN THE MISTS - THE DARK DRAWS THE CURTAIN

"How do you know about Missy Kulver's poppet?" Eldermann asked, now standing in front of her with his mount held behind with a hand on its reins.

Mercy, those eyes...

His green-grey gaze now rested fully upon her and it felt as though she were watching a mountain descend. His stare, like the foot of a mossy slate colossus, pinned her beneath its weight. What she had felt there at the bar of the Flat-Sole was but a taste of the power, the incredible mass, of this working mind that now bore down upon her. It was terrible, but as with most terrible things there was a certain thrill that beholding it being brought to bear, even if she was now the one against whom it was wielded.

"The child carried it with her wherever she went," Regina answered, distantly annoyed at how breathless and small her voice sounded in her ears. "She had it upon her lap everyday as she sat in the schoolhouse."

Within the vast machinery behind his eyes, something fell into place with a near-audible *clank*, and he seemed to nearly loom over her.

"You are Regina Hollferd, schoolmistress," he pronounced gravelly, either a commendation or accusation, and it took more of her will than she would care to admit to not begin nodding dumbly. "I have been looking to speak with you for some days now. Mister Buie has said you were unavailable each time I have asked."

"That is because Mister Buie knows my schedule," she replied, struggling to assert herself upon the conversation which now seemed to pin her where she stood upon the roadside. "He knows I am out of my lodgings before noon, visiting homes and praying with the families. Our watchman has never been one for early rising, especially when a particular inspector expects more of him than wandering the town at night, bottle in hand."

"You do not approve of Mister Buie and his sinner's ways?" Eldermann asked, the last words of the question spoken with a sour sneer.

That little dose of venom somehow shrunk him, peeling back the stony surface of his overwhelming stare for a glimpse, just for an instant, of the corrosion within his great mental engine, a mean smallness which ate him within. He was no longer a colossus. No, just a man with striking eyes and a compelling manner.

"Mister Buie and whatever sins he may bear are matters for him and God Almighty," she responded levelly, at last feeling her feet beneath her. "It just sickens my heart to think that we may not be so utterly at a loss over where the children have gone if our watchman was not habitually drunk on duty."

His spell broken and he seeming to know it, the Inspector stooped and then handed her one of the wrapped parcels.

"You care very much for these children, don't you?"

"Of course." She almost laughed, the absurdity of the statement seeming comical. "They are my students and I wish nothing but the very best for them, and I have grown to love many of the families whose children I have taught."

"When did you come to lovingly serve here in Evynsford?" he asked and then quickly added, "Your accent is not the native brogue."

"Ten years last September," Regina answered absently as she scooped another parchment-wrapped loaf. "I came by way of a governess position in Liverpool."

SUNSET IN THE MISTS - THE DARK DRAWS THE CURTAIN

"Remarkable," he breathed softly, and she stole a glance at him as she looked about for her last missing parcel.

His fierce features seemed to be set into a relaxed yet hunkered posture of observation. He was not grinding and wringing her beneath his driving stare, but seeing her, knowing her in a way both intimate and distant with that long look. She felt that fluttery thrill and decided she didn't need the last loaf.

It was time to go.

"Quite," Regina said and then forced a cordial smile to spread across her lips. "Well, I should be away. I have no horse, and so the trip to the Kulver house will be a longer thing for me. I expect you will have already finished your business there by the time I arrive. Good afternoon."

She moved to leave, tucking her basket firmly under her arm and starting down the road. She kept to the side, all the better to allow him to ride on past her and off to his business.

"You must still be stinging under the barbs of my ill temper," Eldermann observed as he moved to walk beside her, the mare following him by the reins he still held. "That is the only excuse that could justify such a failure in basic arithmetic."

Before she could say a word, he produced the final wayward loaf with a little flourish.

"A pretty schoolmistress travels down the road with seven loaves in her basket," he recited softly, as though recalling a schoolboy's examination. "She suffers a fright from a mannerless mounted ogre and spills her basket. Only two loaves remain."

He stepped forward, the parchment-swaddled bread before him like an olive branch.

"How many loaves will she need to recover to fill her basket?" he asked, his voice nearly a whisper.

With a gentleness she could not have suspected, he slid the offering among its brethren with a soft, lingering pat. His eyes never left hers

Stepping back, he swept a gallant arm to the road and sketched a courtly little bow.

"Shall we?"

Chapter 5: A House of Mourning

Inspector Eldermann was brought back to sobering reality as Jon Kulver's home emerged from the mist like a glowering, hairy-backed crab. They had been walking between Kulver's fields, the fallow expanses doing nothing to dampen the cordial conversation which had grown between Arthur and Regina as they drew near to the farmstead.

In this world of surly fishwives and recalcitrant farmers, the Inspector seemed to have discovered a rare gem. Miss Hollferd was an intelligent and well-spoken woman, and her winsome face framed by her auburn hair was not unpleasant to look at, even in the wan light that served as midday in this blighted community.

She had told him of her duties as schoolmistress when he had first asked her, for strictly investigative purposes, of course, and that had flowed into a conversation about her relationship within the community. Though having lived here for many years and developing a deep affection for the students and her families, she seemed to have no significant friendships with anyone, with the possible exception of Father Weston, whom she discussed in only the most spiritually paternal tone. She intimated that Evynsford saw her as a necessary, if mundane, function of its existence and so would spare her hardly any attention unless something should be disrupted, an event which was rare to happen due to her exceptional abilities and diligence.

This social isolation had not meant that Regina had nothing useful to say in regards to the goings-on of the community, for many children, especially young children, were nearly irrepressible as to the domestic occurrences in their tiny worlds. Miss Hollferd knew which homes were in disarray, which homes were well-ordered, and which homes masqueraded as the former or the latter. She knew whose father or mother drank too much, when they took a hand to them, and whether or not the children were being fed regularly. She knew which parents could read and which couldn't, and which parents thought such things mattered. She told him she would not normally share such things, for that would be gossip, but she judged that such things could be useful to the Inspector's investigation.

Indeed, though he would not admit it to her, Eldermann wished he had made more of an effort to speak with her before his many interviews and investigations of the families. Her insight and frank assessments would have proved very helpful.

It had been her evaluation of Jon Kulver and his daughter Missy about which they had been speaking when they sighted the Kulvers' thatched-roof domicile. Miss Hollferd, her voice dropping to a hush, was finishing the tale of how Mister Kulver had become a widower some four years ago.

"When the horse bolted, Jon, with Missy in his lap, was thrown from the wagon. Mrs. Kulver tried to grab hold of the reigns while keeping an arm about their elder daughter, but it proved no use and with one sharp twist on the stony ground, the beast sent the wagon tumbling. Mother and daughter were crushed between rock and wagon, and the horse itself made

SUNSET IN THE MISTS - THE DARK DRAWS THE CURTAIN

it only six frantic steps before it turned a hoof on the uneven ground. It was a terrible tragedy."

ELDERMANN NODDED, LESS in acknowledgement of the event's sorrow and more because his mind's relentless wheels were racing.

Anger, guilt, sorrow and loneliness; what a potent combination to pour into one human vessel. I wonder if anyone's given it a shake recently.

They came before a low retaining wall that ran the width of Kulver's house and the garden plots along the road.

The Inspector laid his hands upon the wooden post which offered the only passage through the wall of rough-hewn stones.

"Has Missy lived with her father the past four years?" he asked as he lifted the gate latch.

"Absolutely," Regina answered softly, waiting by the wall basket upon her hip. "He hardly lets the girl out of his sight. Every school day he walks her to school and does not leave until she is in her seat. Some days he will not leave, and sits outside like a great statue upon the awninged bench by the road. It was a mite unnerving at first, but he seems to truly love the girl and to see to her, though her hair has not looked better than disheveled for the past four years."

Arthur swing the gate open and then, with what were perhaps the best manners he had shown in years, gestured Regina to walk through.

She gave a little smile at that, and he wanted to believe he saw a slight blush in her cheek as she looked up into his eyes.

"After you, madam," he said with a little, sweeping flourish.

"I wish I could," she said with a little giggle in the back of her throat. "But the last time I was here, Mr. Kulver said a great many things, not all of which I remember, but I am certain that one of them forbade me from steeping across his gate."

Eldermann eyed her quizzically.

"I will wait out here while you conduct your business," she intoned, simply enough. "Just please, when you go in, inform him I am here, as it will save me having to shout at him from outside."

"You must be joking," Eldermann snorted, looking from Regina to the house with its blind, lightless windows.

"Different men handle their grief in different ways," Miss Hollferd stated sagely, though he was certain he saw more than a little anxiety in her quick glance at the Kulver house.

"He most certainly didn't hurt you, did he?" Eldermann asked with a ferocity to his tone he could not explain, even to himself.

"No, no," Regina said with a definitive shake of her head. "Only frightened me is all. I am certain it is only the strain of his fear for his daughter. Please, I don't wish to bring any trouble to the house of the man I have come to pray for and serve."

Inspector Eldermann looked down on the schoolmistress standing before him, and then at the home of Jon Kulver. Images of her racing from that dark doorway, tears streaming down her wholesome face as burly and hoary-headed Jon Kulver roared hoarsely after her spilled from his imagination, lubricating the gears of his mind to a furious series of revolutions.

"Oh, sod this," he practically snarled, feeling a towering, offended rage swelling inside of him as he stalked toward the door.

SUNSET IN THE MISTS - THE DARK DRAWS THE CURTAIN

INSPECTOR ELDERMANN stood in the farmhouse, thoroughly perplexed as to what to make of the man in front of him.

Jon Kulver was a hulking man, thick fleshed with heavy, labor-knotted arms hanging apelike from his broad shoulders. His great head, shaggy with hair gone grey since he was a young man, was bowed over his broad belly as he squatted upon a low stool in one corner of the farmhouse. Clutched in his massive work-gnarled hands was a small poppet of burlap and twine, which stared up into the man's face with seashell eyes.

This had not been the confrontation the Inspector had expected. All his hopes and schemes of uncovering some clue were dashed on the man's utter refusal to respond.

Buoyed up by his fury and conviction of righting the wrong done Miss Hollferd, he had stormed into the cottage, bellowing for Kulver to attend him. No resounding roar met his challenge and instead it took a moment for his eyes to adjust to the gloomy interior and then spot Jon Kulver sitting in his corner, staring at the crude doll. When called, the man did not stir. Only the slow, hitching breaths drawn through his bedraggled beard spoke of life.

Inspector Eldermann chastised, cajoled, jeered, threatened, accused and ranted, but still Mister Kulver remained unresponsive. Eldermann had even gripped him by the shoulder and shaken him roughly, but the man allowed himself to be jostled and then settled back into seat.

A thought had come to the Inspector and then cast about the home, looking for evidence of some stupefying substance to explain the state of Jon Kulver. Not even a small bottle of medicinal brandy lay about the house.

At last, giving up on the catatonic farmer, Arthur called for Regina to come inside.

A few moments later, Inspector Eldermann watched as Miss Hollferd knelt beside the man who not so long ago had chased her out of his home with curses and snarling. Gently, she took his hands in hers and very softly she began to pray.

"Heavenly Father," she began, her voice barely above a whisper, but in the utter silence of the cottage filling the ear completely. "We beg you to meet us here in this place. We are broken and surrounded by darkness. Father, let Christ be our light, and your Word be our lamp in the low, black place..."

She continued but Eldermann couldn't bear to pay it any more attention. Disgust choked him, *beg*, and he swallowed a derisive sound in the back of his throat, *broken*. He had squandered enough of his life in prayer, and he would not waste another minute upon such a useless exercise. Shaking his head, he began to stalk about the house, looking for something, anything he might have missed the last time he was here.

Miss Hollferd's prayers droned on as he checked hearth and pallet, then examined the rough trunk beneath the window. Nothing, nothing and nothing. Eldermann felt his frustration mounting, and more than once his head snapped around to glare at the schoolmistress praying in the corner with Kulver.

Don't either of the fools see what I am doing? Can't they open their eyes and see that I am actually doing something useful?

Snorting with irritation, Inspector Eldermann examined the pantry and then stepped outside to walk about the house. As he stalked about the premises, he spied a small door set into a low

SUNSET IN THE MISTS - THE DARK DRAWS THE CURTAIN

hill. He remembered seeing it the last time he had been here, and he had given it a cursory examination but then had dismissed it. It was the larder, and barely big enough to hold the few shelves inside the wooden framed walls.

Desperate for something to occupy his attention, he moved to the larder door only to discover it was locked. Snarling, he stomped back to the house and yanked the door to look for the key.

As he reentered the gloom of the cottage, he heard Miss Hollferd still carrying on with her useless prayers in her hushed tones. Trying to block out the sound, he began poking about the shelves, muttering to himself as he moved preserve jars and peered between tarnished tins.

"Not as if there are any other missing children," he hissed to himself. "But no, no, let's spend our time praying to empty air rather than doing something useful."

He moved a small jar and it gave the clink of metal on glass. He was taking it off the shelf to discover the source of the sound when a new voice emerged from Miss Hollferd's softly chanted prayers, a voice deep and rough. Inspector Eldermann paused and then turned around, jar still in hand, as he heard his name mentioned.

"...and Lord give wisdom to yer servant Inspect'r Eldermann. Let 'im find the children and ... and l-let 'im find me lil' Missy."

The name dragged a hitching sob out of Jon Kulver, who still squatted upon his stool with Regina Hollferd holding his mammoth hands.

"Father, thy will be done. In Christ's name, Amen." Miss Hollferd finished for him. She gave the farmer's hand a squeeze and then rose.

Jon Kulver stiffly stood up with her, his hairy head nearly touching the low roof. He rubbed the back of one hand across his tear-blurred eyes and stepped toward Arthur.

"My apologies, suh," he grunted with a sniff. "I'm prone to the downs, an' this business with me daughter..."

He trailed off, in an obvious struggle to keep himself composed.

"Quite," Eldermann said, incredibly uncomfortable on several fronts but determined to have the key. "Well now that we are all done wasting time, I do wish that you could provide me with key for your larder. I would like to examine it again."

"Sure enough the key is in that jar, suh," Kulver rumbled, pointing at the vessel in the Inspector's hand.

Ignoring the rather baleful glare coming from Regina, Arthur fished out the small iron key and headed back out the door. Without a word, Miss Hollferd and Mister Kulver followed him out to the larder.

Once opened, the larder proved just as uninspiring and uninteresting as the Inspector had remembered. Dank, cool and smelling of the earthen floor. He was about to slam the door shut in disgust when Regina stooped and picked at the dirt floor by the doorpost.

"Please, share with the class, Miss Hollferd," Eldermann said, unable to keep his frustration from sharpening his tone.

She gave him a scowl, but then rose, rubbing something between her fingers as she addressed Jon.

"Mister Kulver, you don't smoke a pipe, do you?" she asked. She gave the dirt a dainty sniff that caused her face to curdle in distaste.

"No, marm," Kulver answered, blinking in the dark at what lay pinched between her fingers. "Ne'er took to it in all me life."

"Is that tobacco?" Inspector Eldermann asked, stepping forward.

"Yes, I believe so," Miss Hollferd responded, still holding the ashen remains of tobacco between her fingers as she looked down on the pile on the floor. "My nose is rather sensitive to the stuff and I thought it strange that I should scent it, however faintly, anywhere on your property."

Eldermann gave her a quizzical glance.

"Missy never stank of tobacco," Regina said rather quickly. "The children whose parents, or even themselves, imbibe the noxious stuff are well known to me, as the schoolhouse is not very large. As I said, I do not care for the smell at all."

"Someone waited here, in the larder," the Inspector said, his focus narrowing as he felt the impetus of the revelation being brought to bear.

He squatted down and, striking a match from his pocket, examined the ground closely. By the doorpost lay a small patch of tobacco ash, no doubt from where a man had tapped his pipe upon the post to clear it, perhaps part of a nervous habit of fidgeting with the pipe.

Arthur recognized he was making an assumption of a male suspect, but he felt it fair considering the suspect would have had to bodily carry several of the children, some of whom were near on to eight to ten stone, if descriptions fit. Yes, a man with a pipe and who was either very familiar with the area or at least had enough time to find prime observation positions to spy on his quarry.

The Inspector felt a tingle of apprehension run up his spine.

This level of dedication – obsession, really – was something he typically saw only in the most degenerate forms of psychosexual and homicidal tendencies. He refused to pray, but with all that he was, he wished that his dark suppositions were wrong. He could not imagine what else would motivate such kind of actions, but this entire case was without precedent in all of his career.

Before his match ate itself up, he thought he spied a strange print in the earth.

He shook out the old and lit the new to resume his examination.

There!

Just within the doorpost, where perhaps he had rested with his shoulder leaning against the wall, was a soft impression of a boot, noticeable only now that the Inspector squatted right over it under the matchlight. Not of remarkable size and not particularly deep, the bearer was perhaps a man of slight build and average height. No wonder he was nervous. If Jon Kulver had found him, the giant could have torn the man to pieces with his bare hands without a breaking a sweat.

Still, it was not much. A man who smoked a pipe full of a cheap, common brand of tobacco, who was of nondescript height and who was not portly. Given the poverty of the region, that could be naming nearly half of the men from here to Liverpool. Yet it was a piece in the puzzle, and while hardly a complete picture, every little bit helped.

The Inspector was about to rise and extinguish the match when his roving eye spilled over the print one last time and spied a strange regularity in the twists of dirt.

Pressing even closer, he had to use two more matches and endure both Miss Hollferd and Mister Kulver nagging him to state what he had found. At last, sure that he had every detail locked within the vaults of his mind, Eldermann stood and began to rummage through his pockets to draw out a pencil and his pocketbook.

Finding the pencil first, he sketched a wide rectangle in the dirt around the print.

"Make sure no fool steps on that," he instructed Mr. Kulver as he flipped open his pocket book and began sketching.

"But what is it?" Regina pressed.

His sketch of a tangled nest of loops and bars was tugged from the notebook and held up to Jon Kulver, who took it with his face knotted in confusion. Eldermann was already moving outside and toward where his horse stood nibbling grass.

"Take that symbol and gather every man you can," Arthur called over his shoulder as he began to sketch again in the notebook. "In the morning, begin a sweeping search of the ground around the larder and where Missy was taken. Look for any marks matching that symbol. It is not a good chance, but it is something. Also, be looking for strange scrapes on any stones you can walk over. The symbol was made of brass set into the heel of a boot."

"I'll turn the whole town out," Jon growled, a fierce light springing into his sunken eyes. "And I ain't waitin' for daylight."

A glance at those burning eyes and Eldermann did not bother to argue.

"Miss Hollferd," Inspector Eldermann hollered as he took hold of the mare. "Does your vicarage have something resembling a library?"

"Yes, Vicar Weston is quite a-"

"Good enough," he interrupted as he heaved himself into the saddle and then reached out a hand to her.

"What? Why-" Regina began to sputter.

"Please, quickly," he said, those implacable eyes working their will upon her once again. "I need your help."

Her arm rose. He swung her up behind him and then they were plowing into the mists.

Chapter 6: The Tongues of Angels

Regina Hollferd had never taken to such girlish behavior of shrieks and giggles, even when she was a child, but the mad flight to the vicarage had nearly dragged several excited exhalations from her.

The mare was pressed hard and Inspector Eldermann was bent hard to the task, only occasionally calling over his shoulder to ask if they were going in the right direction. They were traveling so quickly through the mist that she was never entirely sure, but thankfully she never steered him wrong. Within an hour of departing the Kulver house, they spied the fuzzy patches of light marking Evynsford proper winking at them through the fog.

Moments later they were before the church, Eldermann vaulting from the saddle to tie the quivering horse to the iron fence enclosing the small flower garden in front of the building. Then he was striding up the church steps.

Regina had to make do trying to slide off the saddle in some form of decorum. The horse's heaving sides made it no easier, but with an effort she managed to land on her feet, her hands pressed to the beast's laboring flanks.

"Poor thing," Regina cooed soothingly as she ran her hand along the creature's shoulder, walking up to where its head hung. "Did you really need to-"

"Vicar!" Eldermann bellowed in his deep voice as he yanked open the church's iron-bound door. "Vicar!'

Regina left the horse with a consoling pat and raced up the steps after Eldermann.

"There is no need to shout like that," Miss Hollferd chided sharply as she came in the door behind the Inspector.

The seriesed rows of pews stretched before them up to the dais, next to which loomed the pulpit. Within the stone walls and stained glass she had always felt an incredible sense of stillness and safety, as though all the world could not breach that sacred peace. Now, though, it seemed Inspector Eldermann would test that solemn security to its limits.

"Vicar," he shouted again, the words reverberating through the gabled chamber. "Where the devil are you?"

"Peace, young man, peace," came the dry, husky tones of Vicar Weston from the back of the sanctuary. "What brings you to the church in such a state?"

Vicar Gerard Weston was a wizened tree of a man, once of considerable proportions but now bent and shrunk with age and care into a gaunt, gnarled figure, testifying to time's supremacy over mortal flesh. Only his dark eyes, sparkling and kindly, testified to the truth that while the good priest may have been bowed, he remained unbroken despite the deep lines etched into his sunken face.

"I need access to your library, Vicar," Eldermann hollered without preamble, moving down the aisle between the pews.

With a shuffling gait, Weston came to the head of the center aisle, leaning on the pew back.

"You are more than welcome to it, so long as you stop all that shouting," the elderly cleric said, blinking at the Inspector. Then he spotted Regina coming up behind at a much more respectful pace. "Miss Hollferd, welcome, Child. Is this excitable young fellow a friend of yours?"

"Vicar, he is the Inspector come to find the children," Regina said gently.

"I am aware of his occupation," the Vicar replied with a nod at the man now standing before him. "But that is not what I asked."

Regina was brought up short. She did not understand the twinkle in the Vicar's age-hooded eyes.

"The very best of chums," Eldermann cut in impatiently, drawing Vicar Weston's curious stare. "Now, Vicar, would you please direct me to your library."

Regina made to correct the Inspector for his impertinence, but Vicar Weston simply waved it off with a knowing smile.

"This way, Inspector," the Vicar said with a crooked, bony finger. He led them through a small door to the left of the pulpit.

Down a small corridor and into a small sitting room they moved at the Vicar's scuttling pace. The room was a bit cramped, with a small table and two chairs in one corner and a pedestal desk in the other. Three doors branched off this chamber, one firmly shut and the other two ajar enough to spy the foot of a simple bed with rumpled blankets hanging over it. The entry to the small kitchen lay on the far wall.

"One moment, please," Vicar Weston said and left them standing beside the table while he disappeared within the room with the open door.

Inspector Eldermann tapped the tabletop impatiently and then drew out his pocketbook He stared at the symbol he had sketched there.

Regina surreptitiously looked at the strange combination of lines and loops, wondering when, or rather if, the Inspector planned to let her in on the significance of the symbol. From where she stood, it looked almost like a series of Gothic letters interwoven into a knotted circle. She had never seen anything quite like it but somehow it struck her as esoteric, something like what she had seen on the Masonic lodge in Liverpool. It was somehow seemed old, potent and a little sinister.

"What is that?" she asked, unable to contain her curiosity. "It is almost like someone has mashed letters into some kind of symbol that is neither writing nor art."

Inspector Eldermann looked up from his notebook, his eyes flashing with irritation, but then softening as he looked at her. She saw something moving within him, not just the relentless engine of his mind but something less ruthless, something softer. She felt some obnoxious warmth creeping into her cheeks as she sent her eyes darting back to the paper.

"Eh, I believe, um, that is," he grunted as he struggled to clear his throat. "I believe it is a symbol formed from Enochian script, a rather arcane pseudo-language connected with the occult."

"The occult," Miss Hollferd breathed, just managing to keep the word from being a gasp. "Father preserve us. What fiendish work has been let loose on Evynsford?"

Eldermann could not hold back a snort at her intense reaction.

"Come now, Miss Hollferd, aren't you a little too grown up for all that? After all, Enochian is supposed to be the language of angels transcribed by-"

SUNSET IN THE MISTS - THE DARK DRAWS THE CURTAIN 49

"By John Dee of London from the visions of the medium Edward Kelley in 1582," Vicar Weston finished with a dry chuckle as he came out of the bedroom with a brass key in hand.

"I see the Vicar knows his heresy well enough," Eldermann said with a wry smile.

"I see the Inspector hasn't forgotten his," the Vicar said with a smile of his own as he moved to the closed door.

Why did he say "Inspector" that way? And why would an inspector, especially one such as this man, know anything about Christian heresies?

Regina kept her peace, waiting for the situation to unfold itself as Vicar Weston unlocked the library door.

"I am curious what Elizabethan nonsense has to do with your investigations," Vicar Weston confessed as the door swung inward.

The Inspector made no reply, his face set at the room ahead. With a shrug, the Vicar led them in.

Revealed was a long, narrow room whose walls were lined with bookshelves that practically groaned under the strain of so many tomes. At its end, the room was lit by a narrow window through which pale grey light poured in. Regina had seen the church's library perhaps only a half a dozen times in all her time in Evynsford. All those times where when she had been looking for Vicar Weston and had come back only when he had not answered her calls from the sanctuary. Even then, for propriety's sake, she had not lingered once she had roused him from study. Sometimes she would ask the Vicar a question in regards to something she had read in Scripture or her prayer book, and he would shuffle back to the library and return with a book. It was an almost assumed aspect of their relationship that this room was his to warden over even if he never openly refused her admittance.

Regina felt a subtle tingle of the forbidden as she followed the two men into the quiet room.

"I believe Smith's *Examining Heresies Past and Present* has a section on the Book of Loagaeth," Vicar Weston mused as he shuffled forward, trailing a skeletal hand across the books on the shelf. His fingers made a slithering sound as they slid across the spines.

"You wouldn't happen to have *Refuting Pantheus*, would you?" Eldermann asked, perusing the books under the soft light of the window.

Regina felt a growing unease, similar to that time when she had made a holiday to visit family in Bath and on the train she had sat beside two French women. Her French was poor when she was in school, and after years in Evynsford it was so scanty as to be useless. The two young women had twittered back and forth, and though she had seen no sign that they paid her a moment's notice, she had the distinct feeling that she was missing out on something important, perhaps at her own expense.

"Is there something I can do to help?" Regina asked as the two men busied themselves, one with pulling out books and the other with quickly flipping through the pages on the table.

Neither man seemed to hear her.

"Doesn't Covell include copies of some Adamic alphabets in one of his treatises against mediums?" Vicar Weston wondered aloud as he dragged a rather dusty volume from one of the higher shelves.

"Inspector?" Regina asked.

"Yes!" Eldermann crowed, suddenly up on his feet and moving toward the Vicar.

"Vicar?" She tried again.

Together the two men, like schoolboys gathered around the latest penny dreadful, turned from one page to the next, pointing and muttering. In fact, their faces seemed to have the same almost lurid glow, though their eyes were pinched with trying to see in the pale, tentative light.

"Very well then," Miss Hollferd huffed, determined to be useful even if the two strangely familiar men were ignoring her.

Turning on her heel, she fetched some candles from the rectory and set them along the table. She had no matches and could find none in their usual spot amongst the Vicar's bare supply closet, but she managed to draw Inspector Eldermann, who was rapidly scribbling in his pocketbook, away from his work long enough to borrow his last few matches.

She lit the candles after placing them across the long table and then gathered the books that had already been pulled. Walking slowly about the narrow space, she placed the books in the open spaces between the candles. The arraignment complete, Miss Hollferd stood before the window, hands on hips.

"Regina, dear," Vicar Weston rasped, raising the book toward the last slivers of window light as he and Eldermann squinted even harder. "You are in our light."

"Boys and their books," Miss Hollferd chided as both men looked up at her from their study. "I suppose it would not have mattered if the very church was on fire." With a wide sweep of her hand, Regina indicated the freshly illuminated table.

The two men's expressions of surprise melted into sheepish grins.

"Lord save us from ourselves," the Vicar chuckled as he brought the book to the table. "Thank you, my dear. Your level head is a blessing to a silly old man."

Inspector Eldermann was already transcribing something from the lighted manuscript to a page in his pocketbook. He then flitted rapidly back and forth between different pages.

"And you?" Regina asked, knuckles still resting on her hips, expectation sharpening every syllable.

"What?" the Inspector asked, bemused, and then his eyes widened as though he was finally aware of the schoolmistress glaring at him. "Oh, yes, well, very helpful of you."

Miss Hollferd's glare did not budge and Arthur's hands, still holding pencil and pocketbook, flapped up in exasperation.

"Are you through seeking my meager praise?" he burst out, frustration adding a shrill note to his typically deep, strong voice. "Honestly, is there something more important than the rescuing of the abducted children that needs my attention? No? Then kindly be useful in fetching me some larger sheets of paper and some writing utensils, or leave me alone to do my work."

Regina was stung, deeply if she was honest with herself, and she felt a combination of anger and embarrassment flushing through her.

Vicar Weston looked like he was about to say something, probably something soothing, wise and gentle as only he could be, but Regina refused to be comforted. She turned sharply on her heel and went to the other room to yank and slam drawers until she found the paper and pencils. She moved to head back into the library and saw Vicar Weston scuttling into the kitchen, but her fury still rode her hard and she marched herself in to slam down the paper and pencils next to Inspector Eldermann. Then she retreated quickly to the room adjoining the kitchen

She told herself at first that it was to see if she could help the Vicar, but in reality she knew it was because as she drove the stationary onto the table, her vision of the room had begun to break with watery distortion. Now out of the library, she swiped a hand angrily across her eyes.

I can't believe I am blubbering like some rebuked little schoolgirl. He treats everyone that way, and besides, he is right. There are things more important than my vanity.

Her diligent expurgation of her tears had slowed her, but then she heard the husky call of the Vicar from the kitchen.

"Miss Hollferd," he called, his thinly white-crowned head poking out from the doorway. "Would you be so kind as to help me make some tea?"

She knew what he was doing, but her anger was only embers now and she knew she could not refuse him.

"Coming, Vicar," she responded with a sniff, mopping at her face as she went.

Without a word, she went into the kitchen, now lit with a few candles and the open stove, as the sun seemed to have set on them. Taking the kettle from the Vicar's bony grip, she went about setting to the well-practiced motions with the pleasant mindlessness of routine. Tea was often a common element in the longer sessions of prayer and counseling they had shared. She probably knew the kitchen better than the Vicar himself did.

Vicar Weston stood out of the way, watching her, letting the pressure mount as he waited on her to steady herself and begin speaking. This was also a function of their little routine. Regina felt the pressure building, and in some small way she hated the predictability of it, but a far larger part of her appreciated the way her minister knew her, her eccentricities, and was patient enough to bear them out. She could admit at least that to herself.

"I just want to help, Vicar," she confessed at last, after stoking the stove and setting the kettle atop. "I feel as though so much is happening that I do not understand, but they are things I need to know. It seems even you, not involved in this business but ten minutes, know more than do I, who at least knew the children well."

"In honesty, it is only my passing familiarity with old books which puts me only slightly ahead of you, my dear," the Vicar said with a stiff shrug. "I still have absolutely no idea as to how Enochian script has anything to do with the why and where of our poor children. The Inspector works at a feverish pace, but he seems a bit uncommunicative amidst all his frenzied working."

"Yes, his mind seems to work at a pace that can't bear slowing down for lesser mortals," Regina agreed, and then remembered the strange, veiled understanding which had passed between the two before they had gone to the library. "Vicar, there is something else I do not know with which you may be able to help me."

"How do I seem to know about this rather prickly Inspector from Preston?" Vicar Weston asked for her as he leaned back and settled his hands over the little pouch of his stomach.

"Yes," Regina said, hoping she did not sound too desperately eager.

"I often get post in the form of newsletters and publications from various branches within the Church," he began softly, looking at her levelly. "In these various collections are often assorted articles and treatises concerning different matters of faith and the ministry. Nearly eight years ago, I read one of the most thoughtful and compelling essays on understanding the sovereignty of God. It was truly exceptional work, and I remember thinking that the young reverend who wrote it was bound for great things in the ministry and our Lord's service. So I wrote to his parish, hoping to encourage the young man, but the senior reverend informed me that Arthur Eldermann had left the ministry less than a month from when I wrote him."

"He was a minister in the Church of England?" Miss Hollferd nearly gasped, fighting to somehow square the two seemingly impossible visions. Eldermann the Reverend, passionate and pious, Eldermann the Inspector, sneering and cynical.

Certainly not!

"Aye," the Vicar said, nodding slowly. "It is not unheard of, as our calling is not always what many a man expects it will be, but when I inquired I was told that he had lost someone, someones, tragically it seems, and that he could not accept the contradiction as he saw it, of a loving, sovereign God and his own pain."

"What happened?" Regina asked, unable to attend to the whistling kettle as she tried to process everything she was being told.

"I don't know," Vicar Weston responded with a grunt as he plucked a rag from a wall-hook and took the kettle from the stove. "In truth, I wasn't even sure it was the same Arthur Eldermann when I heard the name, but when I saw him bellowing in the sanctuary and our eyes met, I knew it must be the same man. There was so much pain and anger in those terrible eyes of his."

Regina Hollferd, rather ridiculously she would admit later, fought not to argue with the Vicar's description of the Inspector's eyes, but then thought better of it. Yes, terrible, terrifying even, when they set on you, but in the way she imagined the saints in Scripture were terrified of the angels. It was a glorious, exhilarating kind of terror to look into those eyes and see – no, feel – them looking back at you.

Vicar Weston seemed to read something in her face as he poured the water into the prepared teapot.

"Careful, my dear," he began, his hands a spot unsteady yet still not spilling the steaming liquid. "My eyes are growing poorer by the day, but I can still see-"

The Vicar never got the chance to finish the thought, as a sharp shout resounded from the front of the church, echoing its way back to them with frightful intensity.

"Inspector! Inspector! Inspector!"

The Vicar put the kettle down and dropped the rag as he made a shuffling advance out of the kitchen.

"Well, this is certainly the liveliest the church has been in some time," he said with less good humor in his tone than his words implied.

Regina and the Vicar emerged from the kitchen in time to see Inspector Eldermann sweeping out of the library, his face fierce and earnest. Miss Hollferd gave her arm to the aged Reverend and they followed after him, but they still fell far enough behind that by the time they reached the sanctuary, the caller had already gasped out part of his report.

"... and without so much as a look behind Jon Kulver goes in," gasped Mister Douglas Buie, his doughy face splotched with breathless patches of red. "Well, the lads with him were not going to bolt down some dark hole, and so they stayed except for young Harry Turner, who they sent to find me. He finds me and I goes to find ye. Some folks say they seen ye flyin' up the church and so here I am."

"I need a fresh horse and so will you," Inspector Eldermann said with sharp, militant precision. "Get us the horses while I fetch the necessary effects."

"What is it?" Regina asked, still supporting the Vicar. "What's happened?"

"Things just became very interesting," Eldermann crowed, flashing her a wolfish smile.

Chapter 7: Dark, Deep Places

Inspector Arthur Eldermann and Watchman Buie tore down the dark road, the bull's-eye lantern struggling to keep its stabbing light out in front of them.

Eldermann crouched over the neck of the sturdy draft horse that had replaced the mare, intent on keeping his eyes on the back of the Watchman bobbing about on the back of a gelding he had scrounged up. The darkness and cloying fog made this no easy task, but he was determined to not waste another second. There was too much at stake now.

True to his word, Jon Kulver had raised quite a party and had not waited until morning. He and his party of hardy searchers, many of them the fathers, brothers, uncles and other assorted relations of the missing, set out into the mist as the sun began to descend. Despite all odds, they had found a strange scoring on an embedded stone near the craggy foothills and, like a hound after a scent, Kulver and company had set off on a frantic prowl into the foothills.

Fortune favoring the bold, they had practically stumbled in the vanishing light upon an old prospector's lodge which they judged recently used. In searching about it, they found a small door set into the ridge face, an old mine shaft of sorts. Apparently, the area saw a little bit of prospecting for loads of copper and tin several decades earlier, but nothing much ever came of

SUNSET IN THE MISTS - THE DARK DRAWS THE CURTAIN

it. After poking about the mouth of the mine shaft, they had almost left when one of the men spied something on the back of the small door, a symbol akin to what Kulver had shown them on the outset of their hunt. Jon Kulver, when called over, took one look at the symbol and snatched a lantern up in either hand, then plunged down the tunnel without another word. For all their desperation, the others could not summon the courage to follow on so narrow a hope, but they had dispatched Harry Turner on the one horse they had brought with them.

Shapes and the wraiths of shapes flew by in the mist and they rode, beginning to climb a slowly rising slope. What the Inspector could glimpse of the landscape grew rougher, more stony. Eldermann called for Buie to put heels to his mouth. He watched the man slow as they entered the terrain.

They could not afford any delays, even for their own safety.

Twin dangers had preyed upon the Inspector's mind as they raced through the deepening dark. The first was that Jon Kulver, in his paternally fueled frenzy, would blunder through those tunnels, where the children may or may not be, and completely obliterate any useful evidence. A footprint stamped away, a chalk sign smudged or any other of the hundred thousand things which could disturb the location, and they could lose any and all chance of finding the children. The other, perhaps darker, fear was that the children were being held there and Jon Kulver had blundered towards his death, and perhaps the death of every single child who had been taken.

As Eldermann had worked in the study deciphering the Enochian symbol, his mind had been ever probing at what possibilities the mark foreboded. Enochian script and other such esoteric occult trappings were often employed by secret societies such as the Masonic lodges and their imitators to add a layer of mystique. In addition, there was no way these abductions had been perpetrated by just one culprit or even a team of common thugs. This spoke of organization, expertise, money, power; all the things that even a father's rage could not hope to match, especially on their ground, if that is what that mineshaft was.

The revolver on the inside of his coat pocket bounced against his chest and the Martini-Henry lever action thumped across his back. The weapons gave him some comfort, but the thought of a conspiracy made the Inspector wish he had the likes of Constable Barty Moore and his finest gang of Brainers to go with him down into that mine shaft. Those lads were what you were afraid of meeting in the dark.

The hills grew steeper and rougher, the road disappearing into a series of worn paths. They were forced to slow down despite Eldermann's anxious misgivings.

The Inspector wondered how Buie was going to know where this secluded, half-forgotten shaft was, but then he spied a ghostly light just above and ahead of them. The will-o'-wisp became a grave-faced man holding a lantern and pointing up the hill where another faint line shone.

Good men! They've made a little guiding chain.

With the string of lanterned men pointing out the way, they soon passed the prospector's lodge and then were bringing their steeds to a halt before the shaft door. Two men remained at the doorway to take the reins of the horses. They did not speak, and Eldermann wondered if it was the night's grimness or their embarrassment at their cowardice which clamped their mouths shut.

Buie pale-faced beside him, Eldermann stepped to the door which still stood gaping.

The Inspector took out another effect he had gathered from his bags at the Flat-Sole, a thick cylinder surmounted by a conical bulb of glass with wiring bound inside.

"What's that, Inspector?" Buie asked after he checked the oil on his lantern.

"A modern marvel," Eldermann said as he made sure everything was snug and fitted about the metallic cylinder. He took the taut leather strap pinned to its length as a handle. He depressed a metal stud near the head of the cylinder and with a soft hum a fist of light punched into the darkness. "An electric torch."

"Well, I'll be bowled o'er," Buie gaped, his fear momentarily forgotten at the miraculous invention.

"It will last us only an hour or two," Eldermann said as he stepped under the door's frame into the mine, adjusting the rifle's sling as he drew the revolver from his coat. "Bring the lantern in case we need it."

Buie moved to follow, gulping down his suddenly resurgent fear. The sound echoed through the dark shaft.

Eldermann appreciated the sound. It helped cover his hurried breathing as they moved into the bowels of the hillside.

INSPECTOR ARTHUR ELDERMANN licked his stale lips with a dry tongue as he tracked Jon Kulver's progress through the mine, ever mindful of possible clues about them or underfoot.

Time and distance passed strangely there in the deep and dark.

At times it felt as though they had just stepped within the mine shaft and followed Jon Kulver's scuffed marks down the tunnel. The shaft did not branch excess for in short recesses easily probed by the electric torch, but it did twist upon itself, chasing the softer earth and stone ever deeper. Winding and descending, always seeming the same dark, timber-braced walls. They could have been down there for hours or moments and still it would have felt and looked the same.

At last they came upon a widening in the tunnel, the walls forming a square room where a few miner's tools leaned upon the wall beside a small pile of broken rock. Some bare-board shelves rested on spikes driven into the stony wall, glass jars resting upon them in two deep rows. No patina of decades-old dust covered them.

Supplies. Someone has long-term plans.

The torch swept to the right where the room opened into another tunnel. Eldermann spotted the small but distinct spatter on the floor. Red to almost black after mixing with the dust on the floor.

"Blood," Buie wheezed beside the Inspector.

The Inspector motioned for silence and then moved toward the tunnel, pistol raised.

The torch drove light down the corridor, revealing more blood, what might have been drag marks, and another twist in the tunnel. Just at the edge of the wall's curve, lying upon the floor, they spied a large boot.

Buie stifled a gasp, pressing obnoxiously close, but Inspector Eldermann did not dare hiss him away. His worst fears seemed to be materializing in front of him.

Too late! Always too late!

Eldermann moved forward, each step measured as he held the revolver as steady as he could.

He skirted the far wall of the tunnel curve, and his light soon revealed that the boot was attached to the prone form of Jon Kulver, his grey hair matted with blood from where something had struck him fiercely upon the back of the head. Missy's poppet hung limply on his belt, watching them with its dead blue eyes.

This close now, they could see that his thick body still rose and fell with breath, but it was a small comfort.

His attacker was nowhere in sight.

Sweeping the torch about, Inspector Eldermann made a decision and then pocketed the revolver head, swiveling this way and that.

"Light your lantern, Mister Buie," he whispered to the Watchman.

He did so. Eldermann unslung the rifle and held it out to Buie, who took it, his eyes bulging in terror in the lantern's glow.

"Do you know how to use that?" the Inspector hissed as he drew out his revolver again.

Buie gave a shrug as his eyes darted this way and that, probing at the edge of the darkness. For all the obvious fear the man was experiencing, his hands had slid competently to their proper places on the lever-action. It seemed that instinct would serve now in place of bravery.

"If you shoot me, you better kill me or I'll return the favor," Eldermann whispered, swallowing the venom in the snarled warning. "Stay here with him while I look ahead."

The Watchman nodded numbly, eyes ever roving.

With a steadying breath, Eldermann followed the tunnel.

For several tense paces he moved along the wall and paused only to check when those shallow recesses crept upon him. At any moment he expected to feel a knife slide between his ribs or some bludgeon crash against his head. He supposed the shadowy assailant, or assailants, wouldn't shoot him if they did have guns for fear of drawing the others from outside. There was always something galvanizing about a gunshot.

The corridor twisted once more. Holding his breath, the Inspector moved around the corner, his revolver muzzle leading the way. He was coming into another small square room. Here there were three cots and blankets. One pack lay upon the ground before one cot. Sketched in chalk upon the walls were crude representations of Enochian script, worked into layered patterns here and there, some so smudged as to be pale blotches on the dark stone. Eldermann felt his skin crawl when he looked at them for too long.

Up ahead was a soft clink of metal on metal and his torch found another tunnel mouth opposite the one he had entered. The Inspector paused for a moment, but the sound did not repeat and so with shivering breaths he moved to the portal.

This corridor led into a single round room that branched into half a dozen different tunnels.

Eldermann did not know which way to go. The hard tunnel floor gave him no clues as to where his attacker may have been and any one of those tunnels could have led him astray or into a trap. His torch seemed to be growing dim, and he knew he would not have much more than a half an hour of light.

He was considering returning to Buie and Kulver when he heard that soft clinking again, and was able to determine from which tunnel it came. The third tunnel to his right.

SUNSET IN THE MISTS - THE DARK DRAWS THE CURTAIN

Cursing himself for a fool under his breath, Eldermann moved to the tunnel, revolver raised.

He was unprepared for what he saw.

There standing huddled in the dark, shackled and collared to one another, were the children of Evynsford. Their heads hanging down from the light that seemed to hurt their eyes, they were pressed together in a pathetic mass of dirty hands and thin iron chains. They shuffled away from his light, clearly aware of his presence, but made no sound other than ragged breathing and sniffing.

What have they done to them?

"Betsy Moss," Eldermann whispered, sweeping the beam of light about slowly.

No one spoke. The children only shuffled a little in discomfort when the torch passed over them. The Inspector thought he saw one or two girls who might have matched the Moss girl's description.

"Carl and Curtis Julep," he said a little louder.

Now he was certain he spied two boys of such similarity that they must have been the twins, but still they did not even look up or whisper a response.

His torch's beam seemed to be dimming by the moment. Eldermann had not forgotten that an assailant was still roving in the dark. Feeling a deep distaste but seeing no other way, he pocketed his revolver, took hold of a sturdy lad's collar and began to lead them back out. To his relief, with a little tug upon their bindings they all followed suit.

It would be slow going, but at least they were moving.

The Inspector brought them into the tunnel junction room and then led them to the sigil-coated room. He looked back, sweeping his torch up and down the line.

Twenty-one. Twenty-one lost. Twenty-one found.

Arthur allowed himself a smile.

Maybe not too late after all.

The defiant thoughts wilted as he turned back to regard the room he had entered, realizing that it was lit not just by his torch but also by a single lantern.

His heart jolted even as his mind raced to make sense of the development.

A shriek, deafening after such quiet, split the air and he had just enough time to raise his arms to intercept something hard swinging for his head. Crying out with a wince, Eldermann staggered back as another blow broke across his hunched shoulders, sending the torch tumbling from his numbed fingers.

"None shall touch the Angel-Washed," a shrill voice crowed in wild ecstasy and another blow crashed across the Inspector's back, knocking him to the floor.

Standing over him was a small, sinewy man wielding a pick handle as a club. His face was drawn back into a manic grimace, ghastly in the lantern light.

Eldermann scrambled backwards like a crab as the bludgeon kept sweeping down, intent on cracking open his skull. The lunatic ranted more about angels, the opening doorway and the eyes of seraphs, but at that moment the Inspector could barely hear the ravings over the sound of his own gasped breaths.

Still too late!

The thought taunted him as, still scrambling backward, Eldermann bounced the back of his head off the wall. The pick

SUNSET IN THE MISTS - THE DARK DRAWS THE CURTAIN

handle came whistling downward. With a desperate lunge, he threw himself to the side, rolling as he struck the other. The club rebounded off the rocky wall with a sharp whack, throwing Eldermann's attacker off-balance.

Now!

His hands working on pure instinct, Eldermann drew the revolver from his coat and tried to take aim, his every movement seeming painfully slow as he felt as much as saw his attacker bearing down upon him.

He tried keeping his arm steady, to draw back the hammer, to pull the trigger, but his arm was still numb from the blows he had taken and everything was painfully slow and awkward. It was almost as if his hand had fallen asleep, and no matter how his mind screamed at it to awaken and pull that trigger, it would not do so. At least not in time.

The bludgeon knocked the pistol from Arthur's numb fingers, the solid piece of gunmetal striking the packed floor with a dull, defeated thud.

Too late!

Arthur, filled with a wild, hopeless rage, found his feet with a speed he did not know he possessed, numbed hands flailing at his assailant. He had been a boxer in his youth, but here in the dark, so near death, it was a far more animal art he employed. He snarled and struck, clawed, raked at his surprised opponent, not intent on winning, oh no, such dreams had left him, but intent on hurting, doing as much damage as possible to his enemy before he fell.

Everything became flutters of shadow and dancing lantern light as the two men struggled. Back and forth, round and round they went, until somehow Arthur sent the pick-handle spinning from his enemy's hands and then his hands were around the man's throat.

Using his height and weight, Eldermann tried to bear down on his opponent and pin him to the floor, but the wiry creature dropped down and kicked up at the same moment. With a cry, Arthur sprawled face first over the top of the smaller man, his grip broken as he threw his hands out to catch himself.

Arthur spun into a crouch, preparing to spring forward when he heard the distinct ka-klick of the revolver's hammer. His eyes narrowed in the dark. He saw the man's pistol leveled at him as he stood before the huddled children. Past the man's darkling shape in the lantern light, Arthur could see that the children's faces were still downcast, as though ashamed of their rescuer's failure.

Too little! Too late!

This was it, the end he knew had been coming and had thrown himself against for so long.

Dying in failure, still unable to save those he should have protected.

The aches of his body were nothing to the pain in his heart, and, yes, in his soul. In that instant before his death, he knew that the years of denial, the years of sneering cynicism, the years of hating what he had believed, were only a blackening, bitter screen thrown upon all that he knew was more than just words.

More than words, more than sensation. It was truth.

Arthur Eldermann melted from his crouch onto his knees, the pain of his body receding from consciousness as he did something he had not done in almost a decade.

"Father," he prayed, his voice rough even in his own ears. "Forgive me my unbelief, forgive me my pride, and now forgive me my failure. Take me now if you wish it, but in the name of Christ, I beg you spare these children. Save them from the hands of evil men."

The man holding Arthur's pistol gave a shrill, almost girlish laugh. "Spare? Ha, deceived one, He has elevated them. They are Angel-Washed and bound for true purity, but you, you are finished."

With clarity which seemed impossible in the meager lantern light, Arthur watched the hammer drop and then the pistol flared – and exploded. A burst of flame, brief but blinding, erupted from the revolver's chamber, hurling slivers of metal in every direction. A few gashed Arthur's face, but most flew past him like angry hornets. The sinewy man, however, being much closer to the backfiring firearm, had his face scorched by the flames and his head and body peppered with jagged shards of metal.

He shrieked as the hair of his face and head smoldered, raising his hands to his mangled face, still clutching the mangled ruin of the gun.

Inspector Eldermann, at first stunned beyond clever action, simply stared at the reeling man's agony, but then he came to himself and was upon his feet. The man's wounds were painful but not mortal. He could still be dangerous.

Arthur had not counted on how dangerous, as the man struck out with the wickedly twisted piece of searing hot metal. Eldermann fell to the floor with one side of his face burning and bleeding.

Staggering but picking up speed, the attacker lurched out of the room, hands held before him. He was getting away.

Arthur struggled to his feet but then remembered the children, still standing there, helpless and stupefied in their bonds.

He could not follow.

A deep-throated gunshot reverberated up through the tunnels.

On the heels of the shot's echo was a pained groan and a sliding thud.

Silence ruled for two heartbeats, and then a voice, thick and nervous. "Inspector?" Buie asked in the dark. "I hope I haven't just shot you."

Arthur Eldermann allowed himself another smile. He took the boy he chosen before to begin leading the children out.

"Thank God for small people," he chuckled to himself. "Small people, small places."

Epilogue: A Rattling Sound

The mist still hung over Evynsford, but when the sun spilled across the sky it fell upon the faces of the missing children. Their heads were raised, and though it would take some hours to finally undo their shackles and collars, the worst of their bondage seemed to be at an end. The fathers and other family members present wept openly without shame as they embraced the reviving youths. Eventually someone had the presence of mind to send Watchmen Buie off to spread the word of the emancipated children. He passed Miss Hollferd in an ambling wagon on his way out of the foothills, sparing only a moment to shout a half intelligible report as he rode past.

The old nag drawing the wagon was sharply spurred into liveliness as Miss Hollferd urged it up the slope.

Back at the mine shaft, Inspector Eldermann sat upon the ground next to Jon Kulver. The hoary-headed farmer sat next to the Inspector, his great, heavy arms wrapped about a small girl with hair the color of corn silk. Blood still stained the back of his head and shirt, while the girl was terribly stained with grime and dirt, but both held onto each other as though there were nothing finer in the world. The father's face was buried in his daughter's hair, but one could just see the silent, thankful tears tracing lines down his dirty visage.

Arthur Eldermann watched them, struck by the beauty and purity of the scene.

Then, as he drew in a deep sigh, he winced, his torn face splitting a little more. Softly he touched the crude bandage he had fashioned from a shirt one of the grateful fathers had given him. It was damp with blood.

Then he remembered the struggle in the dark.

He looked to the open door leading into the darkness of the mine shaft and fought back a shiver.

The children may have been found, but there was still so much that needed answering. The symbols on the wall, the Angel-Washed, the three cots. The men, emboldened by the emergence of their children, had done a belated scouring of the tunnels and found no one else. Exhausted and managing his mangled face, the Inspector had not yet gone back down to search the corpse of the kidnapper in the tunnels, nor search the sleeping quarters. He remembered the pack lying next to the cot and hoped it would shed some light on what had brought these strange, fanatical creatures here to prey on this community.

Regina Hollferd drew her wagon to the foot of the hill below and hopped down to struggle up the rough slope.

She was out of breath and her dress's skirt was a bit more ragged, but how she smiled as she moved among the embracing children and their families. Just seeing each one of them seemed to lift the weight that had settled over her heart. Some of them even took the time to notice her and call out with their bright voices or even break away from protective arms to give her a quick embrace. Her heart sang at those little touches, and prayers of thankfulness poured out from her heart, though she could not find the voice to speak them.

SUNSET IN THE MISTS - THE DARK DRAWS THE CURTAIN

Then they saw each other.

She watched him struggling to his feet, his eyes fixed upon her as he began a stiff walk toward her.

With each step, the weight on her heart did not lift but rather melted, dissolving with every stride that drew them closer.

Some part of her saw the bandage upon the side of his face, the tears in his coat, the shallow cuts across his brow and neck, but all she really knew were those eyes. They were different now, not the same merciless force they had once been. They were still strong, not an ounce of their power diminished, but the hardness seemed to have given way and the cruel sharpness had been turned aside.

Then he was before her, bloodied hands taking her long fingers in his. He looked down upon her and she up to him, and something ancient and deep passed between them. An understanding, a promise.

"I was..." he began, but his voice seemed to fail him.

"I know," she breathed, her undaunted, unabashed gaze meeting his

Arthur Eldermann wanted to say something, anything which would give testament to the titanic events which had begun within his soul, but nothing he could think of seemed capable of rising to the task.

So instead he bent his head and kissed Regina Hollferd.

Deep and soft, bound within a moment of exquisite intimacy and vulnerability, they seemed to float amid that crowd of thankful fathers and jubilant uncles, an unmarked eye of the joyous storm.

Then, with desperate, longing slowness, they broke away from each other.

Her face was flushed and tears shone unshed in his eyes.

"Not quite ready," he said in heavy acknowledgment of what they both knew.

"You have been in the dark a long time," she sighed softly, though the sound was no less heavy for its softness.

"But soon," Arthur smiled, a sad but hopeful thing. "Soon I will come to you."

"I have waited this long," Regina said with a matching expression. "I can wait a little longer."

"Soon," he promised and then they both turned to watch the sun burn more of the mist away from that beautiful hilltop.

BROTHER GRIMSHAW CURSED as he clambered behind Brother James over another rough hill.

'If we had hired a ship," he panted as he adjusted his pack on his shoulder, "instead of trusting a bribed naval officer we wouldn't be clambering over rocks like hares from the hunt."

"Shut up," Brother James growled as he checked the map in his fist. The damned fog made navigation a nightmare, especially as pressed for time as they were. They needed to get clear of Evynsford quickly and reach their master's agents even quicker.

The head of their order would not be pleased that they had been compromised, but the notes and information they had taken might curry some favor.

"Where we bound?" Brother Grimshaw asked after spitting out a mouthful of phlegm.

"Fleetwood," the other man said before stuffing the map back into his pack. "From there we can take a tug to Liverpool."

SUNSET IN THE MISTS - THE DARK DRAWS THE CURTAIN

With Brother Grimshaw mumbling under his breath, the two men slid down the hill and slipped back into the mist.

Did you love *Sunset in the Mists - The Dark Draws the Curtain*? Then you should read *Midnight in the Mists - The Dark Deepens* by Julianne T. Grey!

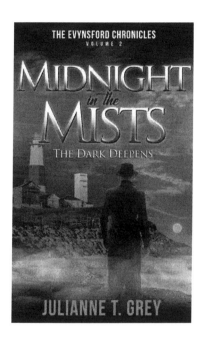

It has been over a year since Inspector Arthur Eldermann was sent to find the vanished children of Evynsford and the fingertips of some shadowy will were revealed. It could almost be believed that whatever darkness had come to that secluded hamlet had been driven off. Yet the mists endure, an oppressive smothering blanket, and as the pale summer of 1899 spreads up the British Isle, another ill wind blows across Evynsford from the Irish Sea.Something has been tearing apart the fields, and so three farmers set out to end the menace. When they don't return, searches begin, and in a prospector's lodge a grisly scene is uncovered. It could not have been the work of any man, but no such creature haunts those shores. The Watchman placates and consoles, but the cries of the widows and the fatherless grow too loud. Something must be done. Once again, things which cannot be explained are plaguing Evynsford and a call goes out for a constable to help. Well, not a constable. Inspector Eldermann has not been idle this past year, his professional triumph and spiritual revival in Evynsford having landed quite a bit more in his lap. Case after gory case has been handed him, sending him wading waist-deep into human depravity even as his soul strives to rediscover what it means to be holy. Wrestling with the black night inside himself and the world around him, the Inspector is called back to the place where his life began its new road. Someone is waiting there for him, and she has been very patient ... but can she and the man she longs to love stand together when darkness comes for them from within and without?

Also by Julianne T. Grey

The Evynsford Chronicles
Sunset in the Mists - The Dark Draws the Curtain
Midnight in the Mists - The Dark Deepens
Dawn in the Mists - The Dark Breaks
Lost in the Mists
Found in the Mists

Printed in Great Britain
by Amazon

42336301R00050